To Sally Britt

The Little Boy and the Birthdays

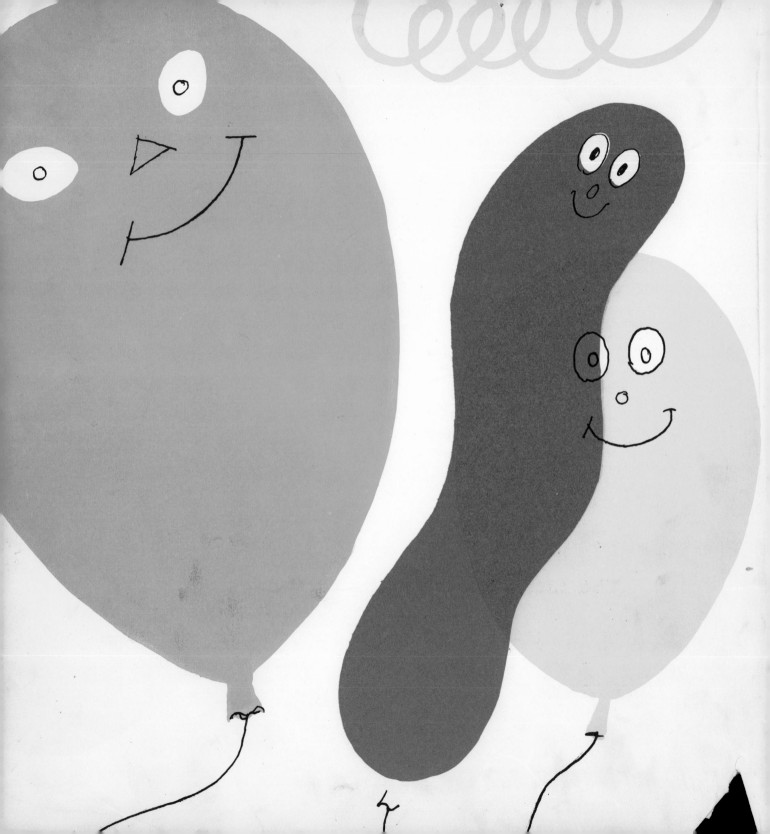

The little boy and the birthdays

by Helen E. Buckley
Illustrated by Paul Galdone

Lothrop, Lee & Shepard Co., Inc. New York

nce a little boy, who lived with his mother and father and grandma, was thinking about his birthday. It was some months away, but he was thinking about it anyway. He said to his mother:

"What if no one remembers my birthday? Shall I tell them?"

"No," said his mother. "The best part about birthdays is having people remember without your telling them."

"But maybe I could *remind* them," said the little boy. "They would be sorry if they forgot."

"Yes, they would," said his mother. "And so would you; but still, the best part about birthdays is having people remember without your telling them."

"Grandma is quite old," said the little boy. "Will she know about my birthday?"

"No one is ever too old to know about birthdays," said his mother.

"What about Aunty?" asked the little boy. "She lives so far away. Will she remember?"

"No one is ever too far away for birthdays," said his mother.

"But Daddy—what if he is too busy?"

"No one is ever too busy to remember birthdays."

"Well, he might," said the little boy. "Maybe we could put a circle on the calendar—that wouldn't be the same as telling."

"We could do that," said his mother. She went to the calendar on the wall and made a big circle around the day of the little boy's birthday.

"Now tell me," she said to him. "Do you know when Grandma's birthday is, or Aunty's, or Daddy's?"

"No," said the little boy. "I am too little to remember."

"But if you can remember your own birthday, then you are not too little to remember others, are you?"
"No, but we had better put a circle around them."

"All right," said his mother.

"Here is Grandma's."

"Here is Aunty's."

"Here is Daddy's."

And she drew circles around all of the days.

"But when is *your* birthday?" asked the little boy.

"I am glad that you asked," said his mother, "because my birthday is next week!" and she put another circle on the calendar.

Sun	Mon	Tues	Wed	Thurs	Fri	Sat
		1	2	3	4	5
6	7	8	9	10	11	12
13	14	15	16	17	18	19
20	21	22	23	(24)	25	26
27	28	29	30	31		

The little boy looked at all the circles. "My birthday comes last," he said. "It's a long time to wait."

"You will be so busy remembering other people's birthdays that it will not seem long," said his mother.

And that was the way it was. The little boy watched the calendar, and the very next week when his mother's birthday came along he gave her a pretty box in which there were two glass beads, a shell, and a little plastic horse. Then he made her a birthday card with his picture on it.

"You remembered!" said his mother giving him a special birthday hug. "You remembered!"

And the little boy was very pleased.

When his grandma's birthday came along, he gave her two beautiful stones he had found and a birthday card with a picture of a little boy helping his grandma to blow out candles on a cake.

"Imagine you remembering my birthday!" said his grandma. "Just imagine!" and she gave him a special grandma hug.

And the little boy was very pleased.

When his aunty's birthday came along, he sent her a painting of beautiful colors and a birthday card with a picture of a little boy hugging his aunty. And what do you suppose? His aunty called him up long-distance and said: "You remembered my birthday! I thought that I was so far away you would forget!" and she sent ten special kisses traveling across the telephone wires.

And the little boy was very pleased.

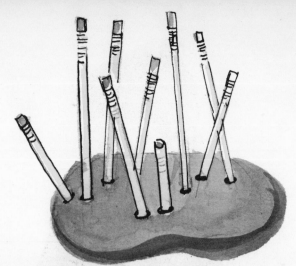

When his daddy's birthday came along, the little boy gave him a large lump of clay with nine holes punched in it and a birthday card with a picture of a little boy giving his father a spanking.

"Well, well!" said his father, putting nine pencils into the nine clay holes, "I've been so busy that I almost forgot my birthday, but you remembered!" And he took the little boy for a ride on his shoulders.

And the little boy was very pleased.

Now all this time the little boy's birthday was getting closer and closer but the little boy did not know it. He had been so busy that he did not know the time between birthdays could go so fast. He thought that his birthday was still far away. He did not even look at the calendar!

And one morning when the little boy woke up there was a box at the foot of his bed that had not been there the night before. He scrambled out of the blankets, and when his feet touched the floor, there was another box! And when he leaned over to pick it up, he could see two more underneath the bed. And they were all wrapped in birthday paper and tied with ribbons.

Now he knew what day it was.

He ran to the door to call his mother, but when he opened it there she was—with his father and his grandma—*and* his aunty!

"You remembered my birthday!" he cried, dancing up and down. "You remembered!"

And he gave everyone special birthday hugs and kisses before he opened his presents.